A DAY WITH A MAIL CARRIER

by Maria Tornito
illustrated by Dean Gray

GRASSHOPPER

Tools for Parents & Teachers

Grasshopper Books enhance imagination and introduce the earliest readers to fiction with fun storylines and illustrations. The easy-to-read text supports early reading experiences with repetitive sentence patterns and sight words.

Before Reading

- Discuss the cover illustration. What do they see?

- Look at the picture glossary together. Discuss the words.

Read the Book

- Read the book to the child, or have him or her read independently.

- "Walk" through the book and look at the illustrations. Who is the main character? What is happening in the story?

After Reading

- Prompt the child to think more. Ask: Would you like to be a mail carrier? Why or why not?

Grasshopper Books are published by Jump!
5357 Penn Avenue South
Minneapolis, MN 55419
www.jumplibrary.com

Library of Congress Cataloging-in-Publication Data

Names: Tornito, Maria, author. | Gray, Dean, illustrator.
Title: A day with a mail carrier / by Maria Tornito; illustrated by Dean Gray.
Description: Minneapolis, MN: Jump!, Inc., [2022]
Series: Meet the community helpers!
Includes reading tips and supplementary back matter.
Audience: Ages 5–8.
Identifiers: LCCN 2021002626 (print)
LCCN 2021002627 (ebook)
ISBN 9781636902197 (hardcover)
ISBN 9781636902203 (paperback)
ISBN 9781636902210 (ebook)
Subjects: LCSH: Readers (Primary)
Letter carriers–Juvenile fiction.
Classification: LCC PE1119.2 .T673 2022 (print)
LCC PE1119.2 (ebook) | DDC 428.6/2–dc23
LC record available at https://lccn.loc.gov/2021002626
LC ebook record available at https://lccn.loc.gov/2021002627

Editor: Eliza Leahy
Direction and Layout: Anna Peterson
Illustrator: Dean Gray

Printed in the United States of America at Corporate Graphics in North Mankato, Minnesota.

Table of Contents

At the Post Office

Rosie's dad is a mail carrier.

Today, Rosie gets to go with him to the post office!

"That's a lot of mail!" Rosie exclaims.

"The winter holidays are our busiest time," her dad says.

5

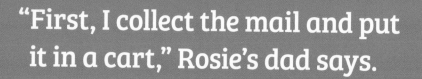

"First, I collect the mail and put it in a cart," Rosie's dad says.

"I can help!" Rosie says. She pushes the cart.

"These shelves hold the mail for my route," Rosie's dad says. "There are letters, envelopes, and packages. I deliver them all!"

8

9

"Next, I sort the mail," Rosie's dad says.

Rosie reads the address on each piece of mail.

Her dad puts them in the right slots.

Then he bundles the mail.

"I organize the mail by street," he explains.

They go outside.

Rosie pushes the cart with the mail.

"This is my mail truck," her dad says. "Let's load the mail!"

Trays of letters go next
to the driver's seat.

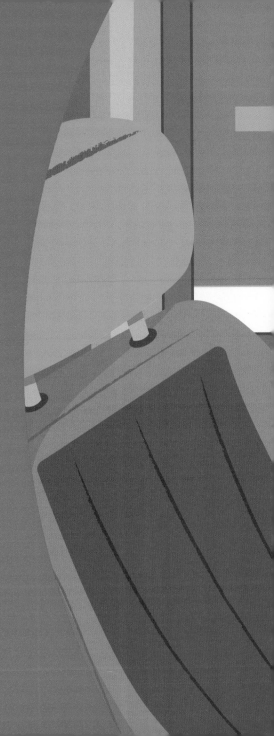

"What is your bag for?" asks Rosie.

"I use it to carry mail on my route," her dad says.

"I park the truck. Then I walk from house to house to deliver mail," he explains.

17

"Look, here's your mom to pick you up, Rosie!" Rosie's dad says. "I have to go on my route now. Did you have fun?"

"I did!" Rosie says. She hugs him goodbye.

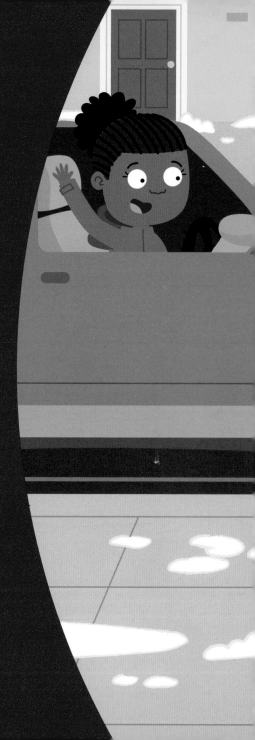

19

Rosie's dad goes on his route. He delivers a big package.

A woman answers the door. "Thank you!" she says.

"You're welcome!" Rosie's dad says.

Quiz Time!

What is the busiest time of the year for mail carriers?

        A. Halloween   **B.** the winter holidays
          C. summer   **D.** Groundhog Day

Mail Carriers' Supplies

These are some of the supplies Rosie and her dad use in the story.
Can you point to them in the book?

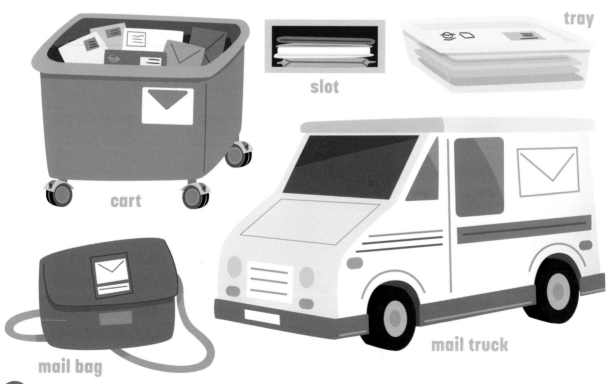

cart

slot

tray

mail bag

mail truck

22

Picture Glossary

bundles
Ties, wraps, or gathers things together.

deliver
To take something to someone.

envelopes
Paper or plastic containers for anything flat, like cards or folded papers.

organize
To arrange things in a particular order or structure.

route
A series of places visited regularly by a person who delivers or sells something.

shelves
Lengths of wood or other hard materials that are used for holding or storing objects.

Index

To Learn More

FACT SURFER

Finding more information is as easy as 1, 2, 3.

① Go to www.factsurfer.com

② Enter "**adaywithamailcarrier**" into the search box.

③ Choose your book to see a list of websites.